Imagine!...
Being
A Tree

Written by Tessa Britany
Illustrated by Brandon Garreau

AuthorHouse™ LLC
1663 Liberty Drive
Bloomington, IN 47403
www.authorhouse.com
Phone: 1-800-839-8640

© 2014 Tessa Britany. All rights reserved.

No part of this book may be reproduced, stored in a retrieval system, or transmitted by any means without the written permission of the author.

Published by AuthorHouse 08/28/2014

ISBN: 978-1-4969-3560-1 (sc)
ISBN: 978-1-4969-3561-8 (e)

Library of Congress Control Number: 2014914841

Any people depicted in stock imagery provided by Thinkstock are models, and such images are being used for illustrative purposes only.
Certain stock imagery © Thinkstock.

This book is printed on acid-free paper.

Because of the dynamic nature of the Internet, any web addresses or links contained in this book may have changed since publication and may no longer be valid. The views expressed in this work are solely those of the author and do not necessarily reflect the views of the publisher, and the publisher hereby disclaims any responsibility for them.

authorHOUSE®

To Nancy, Jaynee, Jack, Jace & Kylee ~
My hope is that you let your imaginations grow as TALL as the trees!... And your hearts fill as HUGE as the sun!!... And that you always, always know, how completely you are LOVED!!!
I love each of you so very, very!
XOXOXO
Tessa
Britany

Imagine!... Being A Tree

Imagine, being a tree . . . Starting so small, as a tiny seed . . .

Then growing so TALL,
all covered with leaves.

Imagine your feet planted in the ground . . .

What would you see
if you looked around?

Imagine your branches,
growing toward the sun . . .

And the color of your leaves in every season!

Is there a child that plays under you?

A child who touches your bark . . . Who plays in your branches?

Is there a family that sits in your shade?

Can you hear their laughter as they rake your leaves in their yard?

What creatures call you their home? I bet you love that you're never alone!

Isn't it cool how the wind makes you move? You get to dance every day, and never have to wear shoes!

Do you wonder who notices how long you have lived . . . Who appreciates you, and the air that you give?

. . . Who takes the time to truly see your remarkable beauty?

. . . Who thinks, without you, how bare this world would be?

Imagine, if you were a tree... And someone loved you, how happy you'd be!

CPSIA information can be obtained at www.ICGtesting.com
Printed in the USA
LVOW02s0815110914

403568LV00002B/2/P